Zara's Eid Dress

Nafisah Abdul-Rahim

Archway Publishing books may be ordered through booksellers or by contacting:

Archway Publishing
1663 Liberty Drive
Bloomington, IN 47403
www.archwaypublishing.com
1 (888) 242-5904

Because of the dynamic nature of the Internet, any web addresses or links contained in this book may have changed since publication and may no longer be valid. The views expressed in this work are solely those of the author and do not necessarily reflect the views of the publisher, and the publisher hereby disclaims any responsibility for them.

Any people depicted in stock imagery provided by Getty Images are models, and such images are being used for illustrative purposes only.
Certain stock imagery © Getty Images.

ISBN: 978-1-4808-8888-3 (sc)
ISBN: 978-1-4808-8893-7 (hc)
ISBN: 978-1-4808-8890-6 (e)

Print information available on the last page.

Archway Publishing rev. date: 05/01/2020

I dedicate this book to my daughter Zara, my
mother Najla, husband Hussain, sons Musa, Idris
and Zayn. You all are my inspiration and help
to paint the illustrations of my book of life.

Every Ramadan is an exciting time for Zara. Not only does she get to see her friends at the Mosque every night and eat delicious foods from around the world, but she can't wait to shop for her Eid dress!

One year Zara and her friend Sana wore matching salwar kameez that Sana brought back from her visit to Pakistan. Last year Zara decided she wanted to wear an abaya just like her friend Noura. However, this year for Eid Zara wanted to wear a dress that was uniquely her own. She wanted something that showed her style, her heritage, a reflection of her culture as an African American Muslim.

One evening while her mother was preparing dinner (iftar), Zara asked, "Ummi can we start shopping for my Eid dress?"

"Zara boo, as her mother would often call her, we have plenty of time to go shopping for an Eid dress. Right now we should be thinking about getting closer to Allah and doing good deeds."

"I know Ummi, but I really want a special Eid dress this year! And I have a feeling it's going to take me a while to find it" replied Zara.

"Okay," said Zara's mother. "If it means that much to you we can begin looking this weekend". Zara smiled as she tried to imagine how beautiful her dress would be.

The weekend came and Zara woke up very early eager to find her new Eid dress. She put on her favorite shirt, jeans and rain boots and was ready to go. So excited to get started, she totally skipped breakfast and hurried her mother to the van.

"So Zara, what are you looking for exactly?" asked her mother.

"I'm looking for something bright, pink, fluffy, and has flowers on it!" replied Zara.

Zara and her mother went to several stores, but Zara could not find what she was looking for! At one store, she found a dress that was pink, but it had no flowers on it. At another store, Zara and her mother found a dress with flowers, but it was yellow instead of pink. Store after store, there would be dresses with only one or two of the things Zara was looking for in a dress. She became discouraged.

Then Zara's mother had an idea! "I know, why don't we ask your Nana to make you the perfect dress for Eid? When I was your age she would make me the most beautiful Eid outfits!" Zara liked that idea and a smile came across her face as she imagined how beautiful her Eid dress would be!

Once Zara and her mother returned from shopping, Zara quickly picked up the phone and dialed her grandmother.

"As Salaamu Alaikum Nana!" said Zara.

"Wa Alaikum Salaam Zara!" replied her grandmother.

"Nana I would like to have a special dress for Eid, but Ummi and I cannot find one at the store! Can you make one for me?" asked Zara.

"Sure, I would love to!" said her grandmother. "What is it that you are looking for?" asked her grandmother.

"I would like a dress that is bright, pink, fluffy, and has flowers on it!" exclaimed Zara.

"Okay, Zara we can go to the fabric store first thing tomorrow morning."

"Hooray!" yelled Zara. She was so excited she could barely sleep that night. She stayed awake wondering what pretty fabrics the store would have and her mind raced with the possibilities.

Morning soon came and Zara and her grandmother set off to the fabric store. The first stop in the fabric store was the pattern tables. On the tables were giant books filled with pictures of people in all types of clothing. From women's dresses, men's suits, children's clothes, to costumes! Those books had it all!

Zara and her grandmother searched through the pattern books to find the perfect dress pattern. To her amazement, there it was!

"Nana! There it is! I want my Eid dress to look like this one!" exclaimed Zara.

Zara and her grandmother got the number of the pattern and searched the big brown cabinets to find the pattern in her size. The next task was to find fabric that was pink, fancy, and with flowers on it. After searching through rows and rows of fabric, Zara and her grandmother found the perfect roll of fabric!

Zara was excited beyond words!

"Abu! Ummi, guess what?" screamed Zara. "We found my dress and Nana is going to make it for me!"

"Alhamdulillah!" exclaimed Zara's father. Zara's mother was happy too that the dress issue was finally resolved.

Zara's grandmother worked during the day to sew Zara's new Eid dress. It was coming along nicely and she knew Zara was going to love it. A few days later, Zara's grandmother came to the house with a black hanging bag.

"Zara, I have a surprise for you!" her grandmother sang.

Zara flew down the steps from coloring in her room, seeming to float over each step. When she reached the bottom of the stairs, there was her grandmother holding a dress more beautiful than Zara had imagined in her mind. It was bright. It was pink. It was fancy and fluffy. It had flowers and it was uniquely Zara's. She had enjoyed wearing traditional dresses from her friends' cultures, but now she had one of her own! This was going to be the best Eid ever!

Weeks passed and it was finally Eid. The Abdullah family dressed in their best clothing and headed to the Mosque for the Eid Prayer and celebration.

After the prayer, Zara met up with her friends. She could not wait to show them her new Eid dress! It was bright and pink. It was fancy and fluffy with flowers, but most importantly, it was uniquely Zara's!

Nafisah Abdul-Rahim has been a teacher for thirteen years. She draws her inspiration from her family and her experiences growing up as an African American Muslim. Abdul-Rahim is a native of Cincinnati, Ohio, where she lives with her husband and four children.